Stinger

By

Eddie J Martin

Copyright 2020 **by Eddie J Martin**

Published in **the USA**

ISBN-978-1-7337495-4-1

Due to the variable conditions, materials, and individual skills, the publisher, author, editor, translator, transcriber, and/or designer disclaim any liability for loss or injury resulting from the use or interpretation of any information presented in this publication. No liability is assumed for damages resulting from the use of the information contained herein.

Here I stand:

I walked out the shower, and there, in the doorway, stood a girl of nineteen, staring at me, average size and height and not too bad looking. You know me. I've been around a long time, so I just stared back. There is no shame in me at all.

She said, "Are you Ruben Kane? Your door was open, and I called your name and got no answer, so I walked right in. Your wife gave me this address and told me you might be home and you might not. She said that maybe you could help me."

"Well, I can't help you in this bathroom and naked. Maybe when I come out…or not." Eventually I grabbed the towel.

She left the bathroom and took a seat in the kitchen, and I went into my bedroom and dressed in a pair of gray slacks, pullover sweater, plaid sportscoat, and my fedora and black shoes. I would be nothing without my fedora. After all, I am a detective. Then I walked into the kitchen, looked in the cabinet, grabbed my bottle of JB, got two glasses, and sat down.

"Can I offer you a drink?" I asked.

"Not right now," she said.

"You were saying my wife gave you the address. How do you know my wife?"

"Around. Anyway, I was telling her about this problem I have, and she told me that you were a private detective and might be able to help me. I didn't mean to walk in on you in the bath, but when I found the door open, I didn't know what else to do."

"The front door was open, not the bath," I said.

"Did you mind?"

"I'm a big boy. I can take it. What about you?"

"I stared because I have never seen anyone as large as you. I'm sorry."

"Oh, that. I get that all the time."

"You do? Ella is a lucky woman."

"You were saying about your problem? What's your name?"

"My name is Gloria. The other night, I happened to witness two men killing a woman. The problem is, they saw me, too, and I've been ducking them ever since."

"Can you tell me what they look like?"

"Both were average size, one heavier than the other, like a prizefighter. All I can remember about the other is that he had an arrow-shaped head and he was dark-skinned. The other was brown-skinned and walked with a limp. The thing is, after they beat her, the person with the long head shot her. Once they did that, they noticed me, and I got out of there."

"Did you call the police?"

"You know they don't do that around here."

"What would you have me do?"

"Get them off my back. They already tried to run me over with their car and push me in front of a streetcar. They're getting closer and closer to wiping me out, and I'm too young to die."

"I take it you've seen the fellows before."

"Yes, I have, but nothing personal, just clubs and on the street. About eight of them hang around together. I'm not sure, but I think they're into drugs and prostitution."

"In that case, these are some serious people."

"What do you suggest I do?"

"If you don't want to go to the cops, I'd get out of town, and I mean right now. Go home and get a small bag and grab the first train to anywhere."

"Maybe you're right, Mr. Kane. I think I'll do that. Can you take me to my apartment and then to the train station? I'll pay you." She took fifty dollars out of her purse and gave it to me.

"I'm ready when you are," I said. "Just give me a minute." I went into my bedroom and got my .38 from under my pillow and my switchblade from my chest of drawers.

"Let's go," I told her.

In the Buick, she pointed the way to her apartment. Right off, I spotted them in a four-door Packard near her apartment entrance. I kept on going. Gloria asked me why I didn't stop. She hadn't seen them. The only thing that bought my attention to them was the guy with the long head; you don't see too many of those around.

They spotted us, and the chase was on. I did all I knew to lose them, but I couldn't do it. Pretty soon, they were right behind us, and then right beside us, and then they ran us into the front of a department store.

I was in and out of consciousness, but I did notice long head reach through the window with a pistol, shoot Gloria in the head, and then run away.

Someone helped me out of the Buick, and the next thing I knew, I was in an ambulance, headed for the hospital.

***

My next view was of Sgt. Johnson of the Cleveland Police Department, asking the nurse when I would wake up.

"I'm awake now, with you coming in here and making all that noise. How do you expect me to sleep?"

"The question is, how you are doing, Kane?" asked Sgt. Johnson. "I thought we'd lost you there for a minute. You feel like telling me about it?"

So, I told him everything that had happened from the time Gloria entered my apartment and what she'd told me about someone trying to kill her after she saw the killing. (I left out the shower scene). I told him about driving her to her apartment, seeing the men she had told me about, them giving chase, running into the department store window, and long head reaching through the car window and shooting Gloria.

"That's all I know. Now, I must get some sleep. I'm tired."

"Yeah, you get your rest, Kane. Wouldn't want to lose you. I'll be back."

The next day, my wife, Ella, came to see me, and she told me how sorry she was to get me involved.

"It happens, Ella. I'm sorry I couldn't help your friend, but she did retain me, so I'll have to follow it through."

"When are you getting out of here?" she asked.

"In a couple of days. It's up to the doc."

"Did you guys handle that Gloria chick?" Mitch asked.

"Yeah, it got a little messy, but we got it done," the Head replied. "There was a fellow with her, but we didn't have time to do him."

"Did he see you?"

"I don't know. I don't think so."

"You don't think so. That leaves us back where we started. Find out who he is, and if he didn't die in the crash, make it so. Take Simon with you, and please, Head, don't mess this up."

Mitch was the boss of the Ravin gang, into drugs and prostitution. He had to kill one of the girls because she wanted to leave, and he couldn't have that, so he sent the Head and Simon out to make an example of her. Some girl who wasn't affiliated with them saw them commit the act, so they had to go after her and eliminate her. It took a little time, but they finally found out where she lived and just waited until she got home. They should have waited for a more appropriate time. They got sloppy, and now they had to go after the person she recruited. It shouldn't be a problem—another problem, that is.

On that third day, 7:30 am, Ruben was released, and at 10:30 that same morning, the Head and Simon arrived at his old hospital room. It was occupied by another, and since they hadn't seen Ruben, they assumed it was him. The Head went over and put a pillow over the guy's head while Simon acted as the lookout. In the end, it couldn't have gone any smoother.

***

When I stopped by the office, Rita (my secretary) wasn't there. Then I remembered that she had gone down to El Paso to visit her parents. She wouldn't be back for a few weeks. I guessed I'd have to get my own liquor and coffee.

The phone rang. It was Sgt. Johnson, and he asked how long I had been out. I told him just this morning,

"I guess you don't know, then."

"Know what?"

"Somebody went in your room and murdered the new patient we think they were after you."

"Hell, I don't know what to say, Sergeant. I guess I got lucky."

"Any ideas who it was?"

"Sure, the guys who killed Gloria. They thought that they'd left some loose ends—me."

"Until we can put a hook on all this, watch your ass, Kane."

"Will do, sergeant."

What the sergeant didn't know was that I was looking for them just like they were looking for me.

***

"Mr. Kane? Mr. Ruben Kane?"

A black man, about five foot eight, walked into my office and approached me.

"That's me," I said. "How can I help you?"

"My name is Philip Webster. My sister was Gloria Webster. I am here to find out what happened to her. Can you help me with that?"

"I can tell you what I know, Mr. Webster. What do you know already?"

"I know she was in an accident and was killed. Other than that, nothing."

"That's true, Mr. Webster. I was with her. After the crash, some guy leaned into the car and shot her in the head. I was barely conscious and never got a good look at him. Earlier, she had asked me to help her with people who were chasing her after witnessing a murder. They waylaid us on the way to her home."

"Have you been trying to locate them?"

"I have, Mr. Webster, but I just got out of the hospital. And you, Mr. Webster, why are you just getting here?"

"I was in the Korean War and a prisoner. I was just released. My release notice was just a while ago. I imagine you have been on the case, since I hear you are a detective. How far have you gotten?"

"I have been making the rounds, as you have guessed. I checked with the cops, and they know less than I do. I have gotten a few bites, and I will let you know if I find out anything. Just give me your address. I expect you will be in town for a while."

"Yes, until I find the ones who did this," Philip said. "If you need any help, you will be sure to let me know, right?"

"You will be the first one on my list."

"Before I went into the military, I use to live in Cleveland, so I know my way around. I do not think it has changed that much."

"What you don't know, just ask me."

"I guess the same old clubs are still there, like the Ebony Club."

"Still there, I said. "That's one of the clubs I will be checking out."

Right after Phillip left, I received a call from Bernie, my policy man.

"Ruben, where you been, man? I haven't heard from you in a while."

"I've been around, Bernie, just been kind of busy. What is it you're missing, my money?"

"No, I've got plenty of that, Ruben. I just like to check on my people every now and then. But I have something I wanted to talk to you about."

"And what would that be, Bernie?"

"Are you after some men who murdered a girl named Gloria, and would one of their names happen to be Head?"

"It may be, Bernie. Do you know anything about these guys? I sure would like to locate them, and you know, they did put me away in the hospital for a few days."

"Well, it's like this, Ruben. You have done a few favors for me, and I did want to return the favor. I talked it over with the guys, and they agreed. The fellows that you're after belong to a gang that runs drugs and prostitution. The two guys are their regular hitmen, and they really don't take no ****, so you really must watch yourself. They have an area here in town where most of them hang out at, but they also have an area outside of town, in a farmhouse. They have it fixed up. Even got a swimming pool in it. Looks like a regular motel. You can't tell from the outside. It's off Highway 97, on the way to Toledo."

"Thanks for the info, Bernie. What you got hot for tonight?"

"I'm liking 642 and 827. Which one you want?"

"I like both of those. Put me a couple of dollars on each one, and I'll be in touch with you. Stay cool, Bernie."

After I hung up the phone, Rita called and asked how I was doing.

"You OK in that big city? If you need me, I'll come back. You know I will."

"No, Rita, I'm OK. Same old thing here. In the hospital for a few days from an accident, a little job here and there, but I'm OK. Enjoy the time with your mother. I'll tell you all about it when you get back. Promise."

"You better," she said.

That night, I found the farmhouse Sgt. Johnson had told me about. I parked a good half-mile down the road and walked back. It was set up about like a farmhouse would be—on the outside, that is, but looking through one of the windows, it was more elaborate on the inside. Modern-size pool on the outside, a large field and barn, with several cars and pickup trucks.

I counted three men and two women drinking at a bar. The women were both white and black, all wearing skimpy swimsuits and incredibly good looking. The Head was the first one I spotted; couldn't miss that head. All had to be part of the gang. I just took it for granted that one of them had to be the other killer of Gloria.

As I watched, they received a call, and the one who took it told the others that the boss had called and said they needed to come back because there was a problem they needed to take care of.

Fifteen minutes later, all three of the men had left, and the women walked out to the pool. It gave me a chance to case the area.

There was a large tree in the back, near the barn, and I noticed a hornets' nest hanging from one of the branches, with hornets flying around. Since it was night, they weren't too active. There were cases of guns and marijuana in one area of the barn, and some farm equipment in the other. The pasture behind the barn held large bull and cattle, plus a few horses. I guess it had to appear to be a working farm.

The girls were having a ball in the pool. Then I had a thought that maybe I'd better look through the house now, while I had the chance. Three bedrooms, living room with bar, couch, and chairs, kitchen with the usual items, marijuana in a few drawers and what looked like cocaine lying about. A couple of .38

pistols in one of the bedrooms, and a floor safe with $2,500 in it. I would have taken it, but I didn't want them to know I had been there.

I stopped by Papa Joe's on my way back for some barbeque, and then I headed back to the office. After that was the Ebony Club. It was getting on 2:00 am by then. There, the first thing I heard was, "Have you heard about the killing at the Rainbow Club? Some guy got blown away there, right in the restroom."

After I had a few drinks, the place was ready to close. Nothing I could do then but go home.

The next day at the office, I received a call from Sgt. Johnson, and he asked me if I had heard about the shooting in the Rainbow Club the previous night.

"I haven't. Should I have?"

"You may have known him. His name is Phillip Webster, Gloria Webster's brother."

"I'll be damned," I said. "He came to see me a few days ago, wanting information on who may have killed his sister. Sounded to me like he was going looking for them. That's about all I can tell you, Sergeant."

"Look, Kane, we need you to come down and see if this is the same guy."

"Will do, Sergeant. I'll get down there this morning."

At the city morgue, I looked at the body, and it was Phillip Webster. You could still see the marks where he had been shot in his head. They really wanted to make sure he was dead. If I'd had to guess, I'd have said that the phone call the Head and the boys had gotten had something to do with Phillip's death. So, first, I had to concentrate on them and then on Mitch, the boss.

A few days later, I had gotten the location of Mitch's home, and I went over there just to see what I could see and what I would have to deal with later. I was thinking it was a large house before I got there, but it was a small mansion, with an eight-foot fence all around the place, an entrance gate of the same size, and a road leading up to the house with a circular drive. The mansion had three stories and a twelve-foot double front door. There were at least three men in and around, with one circling all the time. There were also at least three dogs in the area.

While I was casing the place, Simon drove up to the gate with the three girls in the four-door Packard. They were let in the front gate, and they drove up to the front door of the mansion.

Simon left through the gate, and I followed him. From the direction he was driving, I figured he was going back to the farm. I stayed two to three cars behind him, and finally, he reached the cut-off to the farm. I knew there could only be a couple more men there, so I decided to face it head on.

I pulled in right behind Simon and departed my car just before he did. The only difference was that I had my .38 in hand, and I had no plans to take prisoners.

Simon got out of his car and looked at me, and that's when I shot him in the chest. At that time, one of the other men came out of the house, and I shot him, too. At the barn, the Head was just coming out. He saw me shoot the man coming out of the house, and he also saw Simon there on the ground, so he ran back into the barn, and I ran after him.

Just as I got to the gate leading to the back, the Head came out of the barn with a military-type rifle. It was about as long as he was tall. He started firing, and I hit the ground. The rifle was so powerful that he hit nothing but the house. The Head was under a tree when he fired, and he was firing everywhere. Above his head, on a branch, hung the hornet's nest, and he managed to hit it and brought it down directly on his head, and the hornets went to work.

He dropped the gun and started running and screaming towards the pasture with the nest on his head. Too bad he was wearing a red shirt because that's when the bull took off after him. The bull caught up to him and tossed him in the air a few times and stomped on him. The hornets were still there, but then they started after the bull. It was really a sight. The bull had just stomped the Head, and then the hornets started chasing the bull. You had to have been there. I think they were really upset.

Before I left, I went back to the safe inside the house and took the $2,500 I had found there earlier. Then I relieved Simon and the other man of their funds and departed the area.

That night, I was in the office, counting my haul. Not bad. Not bad at all for one night's work.

***

Mitch received a call from the farm from one of his men. "This is Bug. I'm at the farm, and you won't believe what I found here. Three of our men are dead. Simon, Duke, and the Head. Both Duke and Simon were shot, and the Head—are you ready for this? Thousands of bees stung him, and it looks like a bull stomped him. They're all dead. What you want me to do, call the cops?"

"Hell, no," Mitch said. "There's a lot of pasture out there, and there's farm equipment in the barn, right? You and the guys bury them out there. Call me when it's done."

"Who would do this?"

"I don't know, but we're gonna find out."

"Hey, Ruben. Haven't seen you in a while," Raymond said. "I got a seat open for you."

"Where is everybody, Raymond? I was expecting to get the latest gossip."

"Middle of the week, Ruben. Most of the guys are at work. You need to come in during the weekend. You know that."

Raymond is my barber, has been for twenty-five years. I sat in the chair, and he put the apron over me.

"What's the latest, Ruben? I know you been on some case. Anything you can tell me about it?"

"No, not really, Raymond. It's been dead. What about you?"

"Well, the only thing I have is, have you heard about the boy who got killed at the Rainbow Club? They never caught the ones who did it. You do know that he was Gloria's brother. I heard he was going around, trying to find out who killed her. I got a feeling he found them or they found him. I also heard it was the Raven gang. By the way, Ruben, I have heard a little something you may not have heard. A few of the gang members haven't been around in a while. Some think they were done in, maybe by the brother. Regardless, they are out there looking for whoever done it."

"Who has been missing from the gang?" I asked.

"I heard Simon was one, and the Head for sure. These were Mitch's top people. Ruben, weren't you with Gloria when they shot her? You were put in the hospital over that, weren't you?"

"Yeah, Raymond, I'm still hurting over that one."

"Have Mitch and the gang looked you up to ask you anything?"

"Not yet, Raymond, and I don't think I want to hear from them."

"If they think you had anything to do with their missing men, you can expect them."

***

"Bug, the guy who was with Gloria when the Head knocked her off, did Head and Simon ever finish that job?"

"I don't think so, Mitch. They thought they did, but they got the wrong person. One thing led to another after that, and they never followed through."

"What you know about this guy, Bug?"

"The Head never said, even though he was with Gloria when she got it."

"See what you can find out about him."

***

After visiting Raymond's barbershop, I went around to Cicely's Diner for lunch. A man can't live on alcohol alone. Then it was back to the office to check my mail. If Rita had been there, she would have taken my phone messages, and all that would have been done.

Pulling my bottle out from the desk drawer, I sat at my desk, looked out the window, poured two fingers of JB into my coffee cup, and sipped. Mitch would be my next assignment.

My thoughts went back to the farm, and I wondered if the gang would stay there. I didn't see why not. After all, I couldn't think of a better place they could go; the only big talkers would be the girls, and they knew nothing about the deaths. If they asked where the men were, they could always say that Mitch had sent them out of town. No, I thought they'd stay right there.

As far as the gang itself, I thought I could hit them one by one, though the only one I really wanted was Mitch, the boss. I needed to catch him alone, but I didn't think that'd happen. If worse came to worst, I'd have to attack him at the Castle. One way or another, I'd get to him. It'd just take time, but if they were looking for me, I might not have that much time left.

***

"Mitch, this is Bug. I found out who our boy is, one Ruben Kane, a private dick on the other side of town. He was the one in the hospital when we missed him, the one with Gloria. He also met up with the brother. From what I understand, he may be anywhere around town. The best place to find him would probably be his office."

"No, Bug, I don't want you going over to his office. Black guys in that neighborhood won't do. We'll hit him at a club, just like we did the brother."

"Look, Mitch, let me take care of him for you. I can do that."

"Bug, I don't need no **** at this time. Now, if you can't do it, I'll send a couple of the boys to help you out."

"Have I ever let you down, Mitch? Let me have it."

"OK, Bug, you got it. Don't let me down."

***

That afternoon, I walked into the Raven Club. There was no one around that time of day. Dutch was bartending, and when he saw me, he said, "Ruben, where you been, man? Haven't seen you in a while."

"I've been around, Dutch. You're never here when I come in."

"It's kind of early, but what can I get you?"

"You know I'm a JB man, Dutch, unless you're all out."

"One JB coming up," Dutch said.

After he poured my drink, he took his towel and wiped the bar where he was going to put my drink. He set it down and stared at me.

"Cat's been coming in, asking about you, Ruben, dude named Bug. He was getting very personal."

"Did he have anyone with him?" I asked.

"I didn't see. The place was jumping at the time. You know he's with the Raven gang… I noticed a bulge under his coat. It looked like he might be carrying."

"That's nothing, Dutch. I got one of my own."

"I'm just saying, Ruben. Watch your back."

As I got into my car, I said to myself: It's starting. Are they coming after me one on one? If so, big mistake. I'm assuming they know all about me by now. My office, my home, where I hang out. Bug, do I know him? Small guy, about 150 pounds, bald, always wearing a suit and bow tie. I think he drives a Nash automobile with a dent in the front fender. Has a scar on his left cheek. Yeah, I think I know him.

***

A few nights later, at the second club I went into that night, who did I run into but Bug. He saw me, but he didn't know that I saw him, too. I was at the club for over an hour, and Bug was watching me all the time. I drank my last drink and headed for the door. Bug was right behind me.

I took the road to the highway leading out of town. A few miles out, I turned down a gravel road and reached a barn that I'd used a time or two. I got out of the car, went into the barn, and turned on a light and the radio. Then I went to the bathroom and climbed out of the window.

I watched Bug park a hundred yards down from the barn and walk the rest of the way. When he got close to the barn, he took something from under his coat. When he eased the door open and walked in, I was right behind him.

As he looked around the barn, I asked him, "Are you looking for me?"

He made like a statue and dropped his gun.

"How many did Mitch send after me, Bug? You can tell me. I'm going to kill you regardless."

"Wait a minute, Ruben. This isn't personal; Mitch ordered the hit on you."

"So, you felt you could do this job all by yourself? How many men does Mitch have at the Castle?"

"Five. Three outside and two in the house. He's got a couple more at the farmhouse."

Then Bug did a fool thing. He dropped to the floor and reached for his gun, so I shot him three times, once in the head. Nothing like making sure.

Later that night, I went to my apartment. Ella was there, and I told her that it would be a good idea if she left town for a while. She looked at me and asked if this had anything to do with Gloria and her brother.

"Can't put nothing over on you, can I, Ella?" Then I told her, "Yes, things are going to get hot for the next few days."

Ella didn't argue; she just went into her bedroom, retrieved a small bag, and begin packing. We'd done this before.

***

Pitt called Mitch. "Bug was found outside of town, in a barn, shot to death. They say he's been there a few days."

"I knew I should have sent someone with him when he went after Kane."

"You think Kane did him in?"

"I bet money on it," said Mitch. "Now I'm thinking he also took out Simon and the Head."

"What you want to do about it?"

"We got to find him and take care of him. If we let him get away with this, we'll lose all respect, and we'd just as well give it up and leave town. Tell you what, Pitt. Find him and mess him up bad. The Bug found out where he lives and hangs out. Take as many men as you need."

"Me and a couple more men should do. Yeah, Mitch, we'll start looking tonight."

***

Ebony Club, Rainbow Club, Rooster Tail Club, Standalone Club, One-Night Stand Club, and Boomerang Club. By three in the morning, Pitt and two others decided to give it up for the night and went back to the Castle. I was watching. I called it a night, too.

***

Pitt and the other two went back out the very next night at 2:00 in the morning at the Rooster Tail. After splitting up, one of the men saw Kane and decided to go after him alone. In the bathroom, he confronted Kane, but it didn't work out well for him. An hour later, Pitt found him in the toilet with his throat cut. He called Mitch and told him what had happened.

"Looks like while we're hunting him, he's hunting us."

"Come back to the Castle, and we'll come up with another plan," said Mitch.

***

On the way back to the Castle, I followed them. In a secluded part of town, I drove up beside them and ran them off the road, into a tree. Both men were hurt. One man's body had gone through the windshield, and the vehicle was heavily damaged.

Gas was flowing in and around the vehicle, and I threw a match and ignited it. It went up immediately, and I noticed one of the men wasn't dead and was trying to get out, but the fire took hold of him, and all I could hear was screaming.

***

That morning, Mitch asked one of his men, "What time did Pitt and the boys get back last night?"

"They're not back yet," he was told.

"That don't sound right. We'll wait a while. Maybe they got him."

The gate called Mitch and said that there were two cops there to see him. "Let them in," Mitch said.

The cops came to the door, and one said to Mitch, "I'm sorry to inform you, but a couple of your men were in an accident not too far away, and both are dead."

Mitch thanked the cops, and both went away.

"Accident, my ***. That wasn't no accident. Kane got to them. I'd bet on it."

Mitch went back into the house and started throwing furniture around until he got tired, and then he got mad. "Six men. He has taken six men from me, and I won't let him get away with it."

Mitch called the two men he had at the farmhouse and told them to go after Kane, find him, and kill him. "Go to his office and his apartment and wherever else that he may be in town. I want you to search the town over. Find him."

The two men left at the Castle, he wanted to get out and search also. "But Mitch," one said, "that will leave you with no protection, only the girls and the dogs outside."

"I've got five guns, and I know how to use them. Let him come this way. I got something for him."

***

The two men left the farmhouse, and I moved in. I figured the best place for me would be at the farm since the girls were gone and the two men stationed there were looking for me, so no one was left. It was the last place they would look.

I walked in and checked out the house, and then the barn just to make sure; I didn't want any surprises. I walked through the kitchen, and my stomach started talking to me. I looked in the fridge and found that it was packed: ham, steaks, fried chicken, and at least two six-packs of beer. I took out a drumstick and a beer. I was feeling alright after that.

I looked around where I had found that $2,500, but there was nothing there. Then I returned to the barn to look for the cases of weapons, but only one was left, with a few rifles and handguns. I took a couple of them. Oh, what the hell, I thought, and took them all. I took the weapons out to my car, came back, and got myself another beer.

***

Mitch's men had covered the town twice. They met up at the Rainbow club to decide what they were going to do next and see if they had missed something. They called Mitch, and he told them to stay out, even if it took all night.

"Did you check out his office and home? If so, check again. What about a girlfriend? Did you all check on her?"

"I didn't know he had a girlfriend," Pitt said, "just a wife."

"He's a private detective. All those guys have a woman or two. Check that out."

Pitt and the men arrived at Freda's apartment. They knocked on the door, and she opened it.

"Yeah?" she said.

"We're looking for Ruben Kane. He here?" said Pitt.

"No. I haven't seen him in six months or more."

Pitt pushed his way in, and the men followed. "Where is he?"

"I have no idea," Freda said.

Pitt slapped her, knocking her to the floor. She stayed there for a moment but then started to get up. Once she was up, Pitt asked her again where Kane was, but she didn't answer. He slapped her again, knocking her to the floor, and then he got down on one knee and asked her again. She said she did not know. He stood up and told his men to convince her. After beating on her, he had the men stop, and he told Freda to let them know when she heard from him.

The next location they went to, the girl wasn't home, so they trashed the apartment and left. They went back over to Ruben's office and his apartment, but no Kane.

***

Meanwhile, I was at the farm, sitting on the couch with a beer, watching a sitcom on TV. I started to go swimming, but I didn't want to be caught with my pants down, so to speak. I called Raymond at the barbershop to find out the latest. He informed me that Freda was in the hospital.

"A few of Mitch's men put her there. They were looking for you. Matter of fact, I heard guys been looking for you all over town. Ruben, you better get on top of whatever you are into, and quick."

"Thanks, Raymond. I'll be talking to you. If they don't find me in the city, they'll be coming back here to the farm, and I'll be waiting.

***

Pitt told Mitch that Ruben was nowhere to be found. "He's gone underground, nowhere to be seen."

"We'll wait him out," Mitch said, "and when he does come out, we'll be waiting for him. Send the men who were at the farm back to continue the job they were working on. We'll have to hire a few more men for the Castle."

"What about the girls?" asked Pitt. "Send them back to the farm with the guys?"

"Sounds good to me. I'm getting tired of them."

***

I set up the rifle so it was pointing out the kitchen window, toward the front gate. I would get them as they stepped out the car; no sense waiting. The girls, I had no quarrel with, so I'd just leave them alone.

The girls got out of the car first, and with no hesitation, they started racing toward the pool, taking off their clothes as they ran. The men were next, taking their time as they got close to the front door. That's when I turned loose on them. That was a hell of a shot, if I must say. Two head shots. They went down like big game in Africa. The girls never heard a thing; they were too busy having fun.

***

As I was leaving the house, the phone rang. I picked it up.

"Hello."

"Who is this?" asked Mitch.

"Who is this?"

"Goddamnit, you know who this is. I'm just checking to see if you guys got back. Have you seen Kane yet?"

"Yeah, we've seen him."

"Where is he at?"

"I'm right here talking to you, Mitch."

"You, you, who is this?"

"This is Ruben Kane. You wanted to talk to me?"

"You *******! You over at the farmhouse! What did you do with my men?"

"You know what I did with them, Mitch, and I'll be coming for you next."

"Kane, Kane, I'm going to kill your ***! You can bet on that. I'm going to hurt you. I'm going to skin you alive. I'm going to skin your momma alive. Do you understand me? This is war, and I mean that."

"I'll be coming for you, Mitch," I said, and then I hung up.

***

An hour later, Mitch and two of his men drove into the gate of the farmhouse. The men were still lying on the ground, and the girls were still in the pool, having fun. Mitch jumped up and down in frustration. Then he ran over to the pool, cursed the girls out, and told them to get off his property and that he never wanted to see them again.

He gave them one of the cars, and when they made mention of going back to the Castle, Mitch said, "Hell, no. Didn't I tell you I don't want you anywhere around? Look at my men. And you didn't hear a damn thing. Get the **** out of my sight."

Mitch told the other men to start burying the dead ones. He was going back to the Castle.

***

A few nights later, in the compound of the Castle, two of the guards were talking.

"Look here, babe. I've been thinking about this. Six of our men have been knocked off by this Kane guy. I have to tell you, I'm thinking he's rather good. The way it's going, we'll be next. There's not enough money in the world worth us being knocked off, plus I've got a date tomorrow night."

"So, what are you saying, to get out of Dodge?"

"That's what I'm saying, and get out right now. Mitch's got the dogs and one guy in the house. That should do him. There's nothing holding us back. What do you say?"

"I say you're right. Let's get."

***

Two hours later, I was at the back gate with a handful of hamburger meat with some good stuff inside, and I threw each dog a handful and waited. Fifteen minutes later, the dogs were all quiet and lying down. I climbed over the fence and walked through the back door, easy. No one was around, though I did hear music in the upstairs bedroom.

I headed that way. On my way up the stairs, a person came out of one of the rooms, saw me, and pulled a gun and fired. I had no choice but to put him down. I'd wanted to slip in on Mitch, but that was a loss now. The man fell down the stairs, and I wasted no time in getting up there and past him.

I walked up to the door where the music was coming from, placed myself to the side of the door, and turned the knob. I fired five shots through the door, two where the lock was, and the door flew open.

I was just in time to see Mitch jump out the patio window and down to the ground, and I hoped he broke a leg or something. When I looked down, I saw him limping away. I fired a few shots at him, but I missed.

I ran down the stairs and out the front door just in time to see him driving out of the garage and then out through the gate. My car was in back. No way to catch him now.

Before I left, I went through the house and found cash and jewelry. I took it all; they wouldn't need it anymore.

***

Mitch didn't stop in Cleveland. He didn't stop in Chicago. He kept going until he reached Oklahoma, where he decided to settle down. It was out of the way, and Kane would never find him there.

***

In a week's time, everything was back to normal. Ella, my wife, was back home. Rita, my secretary, was back at the office, and my girlfriend was back, even though she was still mad at me. Everything was back to normal.

The End

Other Books by This Author

Enlisted at 14…A Memoir

Enlisted at 14…And the Journey Continues

Enlisted at 14…Looking Back

Willow…A Novel

Willow…One for the Team

Willow…And the Medusa

Little Miss Willow…A Short Story

Assassin

Blacker the Berry

Meet Ruben Kane

R.K. {Ruben Kane}

Ruben's Bag

Ruben's Bad Side

Smooth…A Ruben Kane novel

Mo Kane

Here 'Tis

And Then Some

Dear Client

Ducks in a Row

Just a Dream

Dream Catcher

Beyond the curve

First One In

Switch

Dumas…Outrageous

Well, I'll be

Redemption

Senior Kane

That Night

Black Russian

Medusa Untamed

Snuggle Puss

Too Much Kane